Classic Literature

W9-BHA-034

The Prince and the Pauper

by
Mark Twain

retold by
Alan Venable and Jerry Stemach

Don Johnston Incorporated
Volo, Illinois

Edited by:
Jerry Stemach, MS, CCC-SLP
Speech Language Pathologist, Director of Content Development, Start-to-Finish TM Books

Gail Portnuff Venable, MS, CCC-SLP
Speech Language Pathologist, San Francisco, California

Dorothy Tyack, MA
Learning Disabilities Specialist, San Francisco, California

Consultant: Ted S. Hasselbring, PhD
William T. Brian Professor of Special Education Technology, University of Kentucky

Copy Editor: Susan Kedzior

Cover Design and Illustration: Susan Baptist, Karyl Shields, Jeff Ham

Interior Illustrations: Jeff Ham

Read by: Nick Sandys

Audio Producer: Mark Blottner

Sound Engineer: Tom Krol, *TK Audio Studios*

Copyright © 2000 Start-to-Finish™ Publishing. All rights reserved.
Reprint #1, 2002.

The Don Johnston logo and Start-to-Finish™ are trademarks of Don Johnston Incorporated. All rights reserved.

Published by:

Don Johnston Incorporated
26799 West Commerce Drive
Volo, IL 60073
800.999.4660 USA Canada
800.889.5242 Tech Support
www.donjohnston.com

DON JOHNSTON

Printed in the U.S.A. No part of this publication may be reproduced, stored in a retrieval system or transmitted in any form or by any means electronic, mechanical photocopying recording, or otherwise.

International Standard Book Number
ISBN 1-58702-361-X

Contents

About the Reader

Nick Sandys is a member of Actors' Equity Association and AFTRA and has performed in theaters in Chicago, New York, Dallas/Fort Worth, London, England and Edinburgh, Scotland as well as lending his voice to numerous commercials. He is also a certified Fight Director with The Society of American Fight Directors and is the resident combat choreographer at The Lyric Opera of Chicago and at The Theater School at DePaul University. Nick holds an MA in English Literature from Cambridge University and is currently PhD(ABD) at Loyola University Chicago. He grew up in the ancient city of York, in the north of England.

Chapter 1
The Prince and
the Pauper are Born

About 450 years ago, in England, two boys were born on the same day. One boy was born into a poor family named Canty, and nobody wanted him. The other boy was born into a rich family named Tudor, and everyone wanted him very much.

Tom Canty was born in a poor house in London that was called Offal Court. The word "offal" means the guts of a dead animal. If you think that Offal Court sounds like an awful place, you're right! It was awful.

Tom's parents were paupers. This meant that they were very poor. They were too poor to take care of their children. Tom and his sisters had to sleep on a dirty floor, and they never had enough food to eat.

When Tom Canty was born, his father said, "What's he good for? Who needs another pauper? He's just one more hungry mouth to feed!"

The other boy was named Edward Tudor, and he was the son of King Henry the Eighth. Everyone in England had been waiting for the new Prince to be born.

The people of London danced in
the streets when they heard the news.
They shouted, "Edward Tudor,
Prince of Wales! Someday he will
be King of England!"

The years went by. Now, Edward
and Tom were ten years old. Edward
was a prince in the castle, and Tom
was a pauper in Offal Court.

Tom's father, John Canty, was
a thief and a bully. He got drunk
whenever he had any money. He made
Tom beg for money from people on
the street.

If Tom didn't bring any money home, his father would beat him. Tom was always hungry. His mother tried to help Tom, but she didn't have anything to give him.

There were other people living in Offal Court as well. One of them was a poor old priest named Father Andrew. Father Andrew had lived and worked in the royal palace many years before, and so he could tell Tom all about life in the palace.

He told Tom stories about how kings
and princes lived. Father Andrew also
taught Tom how to read and write.

Tom dreamed about being a prince
and living in a palace. When he played
outside with his friends, he always
said to them, "I'll be the Prince, and
you be the noble men and women
in my court."

"But we are playing in the mud,"
his friends would say.

"This is not mud," Tom would
answer. "This is our royal palace!"

For a little while, these games would make them forget that they were poor and hungry.

As time went by, Tom wanted more and more to see a real prince. One day, he walked outside London and came to a palace. There was a crowd of people outside the palace gates. They were watching a boy who was playing behind the fence. The boy wore beautiful silk clothes. His belt and dagger were covered with jewels.

"That must be a prince!" thought Tom to himself, as he walked up to the fence.

He was right. It was Prince Edward himself.

There were guards outside the gate. When they saw Tom standing near the fence, they grabbed him and threw him onto the ground.

"Get away from here, you little beggar!" they shouted.

The crowd of people laughed at Tom.

The Prince ran up to the guards at the gate. "Don't treat this boy that way!" he cried. "Open the gates and let him in!"

Suddenly, the crowd stopped laughing. They took off their hats and bowed and said, "Long live the Prince of Wales!"

The guards also bowed, and opened the gates.

The Prince held out his hand to Tom. "Come with me," said the Prince. "You look hungry."

"Could I be dreaming?" Tom asked himself. But he was not dreaming. Before he knew it, Tom was inside the Prince's own room in the palace.

Chapter 2

The Prince
Becomes a Pauper

The Prince sent for food. Tom had seen food like this in one of Father Andrew's books, but Tom had never tasted this kind of food himself.

"What is your name?" asked the Prince.

"Tom Canty, sir," said Tom.

"Do you have parents?" asked the Prince.

"Yes," Tom answered.

"Are they good to you?" asked the Prince.

"My mother is good to me," replied Tom. "But my father beats me."

The Prince was angry when he heard this. "Do your servants do what you tell them to do?" he asked.

"Servants?" Tom replied. "I don't have any servants!"

"Then who helps you to get dressed in the morning?" asked the Prince. "Who washes you?"

Tom laughed. "Why should I take off my clothes?" he asked. "These are the only clothes that I have. And why should I wash? I play in the river!"

The Prince had never met a pauper before, and he wanted to know all about Tom's life. Tom told him about fighting with other boys, swimming in the river, and playing in the mud.

"That sounds wonderful!" said the Prince. "Just once in my life, I wish that I could put on your old clothes, and roll around in the mud! I would give up being King for that."

Tom looked at the Prince and said, "I wish that I could wear fine clothes like yours."

Then the Prince had an idea. "Let's trade clothes, and see how we look!" he said.

So Tom put on the Prince's fine clothes, and the Prince put on Tom's rags. Then they looked at themselves in the mirror. What a surprise! Their hair was the same color. Their eyes were the same color. They were exactly the same size.

In fact, they looked like twins! The only difference was their clothes.

The Prince looked at his new friend from head to toe. "Tell me," said the Prince. "How did you get that red mark on your hand?"

"The guard outside the gate pushed me down," Tom replied.

Prince Edward was furious. "How dare he do that to you! I will have him punished," said the Prince. "Wait here until I get back."

Just before he rushed out the door, the
Prince grabbed something from
the table and hid it.

Then the Prince ran outside.
"Open these gates!" he commanded
the guards.

These guards were the same ones
who had pushed Tom to the ground.
As soon as they opened the gates,
they grabbed the Prince and threw
him to the ground.

"Take that, you little beggar!"
they cried.

The Prince was full of rage. He got up and shouted, "I am Edward, Prince of Wales! You will die for even touching me!"

The guards laughed. Then the crowd laughed. The Prince began to run. "He's running back to London," said one man.

"Make way for the Prince of the Paupers!" shouted another man.

"I am the Prince of Wales!" the Prince insisted. The crowd only laughed as they chased after him.

Prince Edward ran so far that his feet began to bleed. He knew that he was in London, but he was quite lost. He wanted to find Offal Court, but it was dark now, and it began to rain.

Suddenly, a man grabbed the Prince by his neck. The man was holding a club in his other hand.

"Where have you been, Tom Canty?" the man shouted. "I'm your father and I'm waiting for my money. Where's my money from your begging? Give it to me or I'll break every bone in your body!"

"Are you really Tom's father?" asked the Prince.

"I don't have time for your crazy games, Tom," said the man.

"I am not Tom!" the Prince cried. "I am the Prince of Wales! Take me back to the palace! My father, the King, will give you money!"

Tom's father shook his head and laughed. "You *have* gone crazy!" he shouted. He grabbed the Prince by the neck again and dragged him away toward Offal Court.

Just then, an old man stepped up and blocked the road. "John Canty!" the old man commanded. "Take your hands off that boy!"

Tom's father lifted his club in the air. "Mind your own business," he said. Then he hit the old man on the head. The old man groaned and fell down in the road.

Chapter 3

Deeper in Trouble

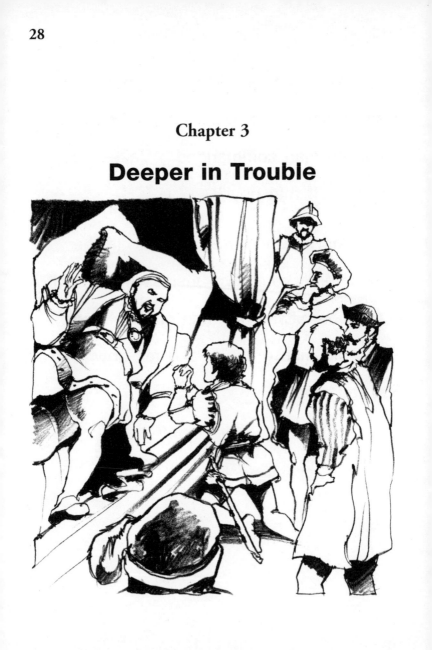

Tom was still in Prince Edward's room at the palace. Tom was pretending that he was the Prince now. He sat in Edward's chairs and played with Edward's sword and dagger. But soon, Tom began to worry. What if someone found him in the Prince's room, and then killed him for stealing the Prince's clothes?

While Tom was worrying about this, the door opened and a servant came in and bowed to him. "Lady Jane Grey is here to see you," said the servant.

Tom expected to see a woman, but a sweet, young girl came into the room instead. "What's the matter?" she asked. "Why are you so pale?"

Tom knew by her clothes that Lady Jane must be a princess, so he got down on his knees.

"Have pity on me!" he begged. "I am not the Prince. I am Tom Canty of Offal Court. Please help me get my rags back and let me go home."

Lady Jane was amazed. "My lord, you are acting so strange!" she said. Then she ran out and told people in the hallway about the Prince.

"The Prince is going mad!" they whispered to each other. "He thinks that he is a pauper!"

Tom decided to run away. He opened the door and walked into the hallway. The servants and noblemen all bowed to him as he walked by. At the end of the hallway, there was a large room that was filled with people.

They were all standing around a bed.
An old man with grey hair and a grey
beard was lying on the bed. His face
looked tired and pale. The old man
looked up and spoke to Tom.

"My son! My prince!" the old man
said. "What are these rumors that
I hear about you? People say that
you are going mad!"

It was Prince Edward's father,
King Henry the Eighth!

Tom got down on his knees.
"Please don't let them kill me, sir!"
he begged.

The King was amazed. "Don't you even know your own father?" he asked. "Don't you know that I love you? I would never let anyone hurt you!"

"But I am not your son," said Tom. "I am just poor Tom Canty from Offal Court. This is all a mistake! Please, let me go home!"

Now the King *really* began to worry.

"Hear me," the King commanded. "The Prince has been studying too hard. Take away all of his books and teachers! No more studying! Let the Prince play games until he feels better," said the King. "Pretend that everything is fine, and maybe he will get well soon."

Tom was worried as he left the King. The King and his men were not going to let Tom leave the palace, and they were not going to leave him alone. What was he going to do?

Tom was taken to a room that was filled with servants. In this room was a beautiful table with one chair. One servant helped Tom to sit down at the table. Another servant unfolded a napkin. Tom held up the napkin and asked, "What is this for?" He picked up the food and ate it with his fingers.

After dinner, there was a bowl of nuts on the table, and Tom poured the nuts into his pocket so that he could eat them later. Everything that Tom did was wrong, but the servants pretended not to see his mistakes.

When Tom went back to Edward's bedroom, one of the Prince's uncles came to see him. This uncle was the Earl of Hertford. Like everyone else, he thought that Tom was really the Prince.

"Let me help you remember how to act like a prince," said the Earl. "Never bow to anyone. If you want someone to go away, wave your hand. If you cannot remember the names of your friends, pretend that you remember. I will stay near you and help you," said the Earl.

Tom was a fast learner. "If I can *act* like a prince, maybe they won't kill me after all," he thought to himself.

"Now, you must rest for a while, Your Highness," said the Earl. "Tonight you must go to an important dinner at the Guildhall in London!"

Chapter 4

The Prince at Guildhall

Meanwhile, John Canty had taken the real Prince to a cold, dirty little room in Offal Court. In the candlelight, the Prince saw two women and two girls in the room. These were Tom's two sisters, and his mother and grandmother. The Prince also saw that there was no food and no fire, and the only place to sleep was on the floor.

"Tell us your name," commanded Tom's father.

The Prince said, "I am Edward, Prince of Wales."

Tom's mother said, "No, Tom, don't say that! Your father will beat you!"

The Prince looked at her and said, "Your son, Tom, is not crazy. Take me back to the palace and I will show him to you."

John Canty got angry again. He began to beat the Prince. Tom's mother was holding the Prince in her arms, so John Canty beat her, also. "Stop it!" cried Tom's mother. But he kept beating them until he was too tired to hit them any more.

Tom's mother stayed awake and worried all night long. What was wrong with Tom? Why was he acting so strange? Could this be a mistake?

The Prince was worried, too. He was worried about Tom's poor mother and sisters. He was worried about escaping from John Canty.

Suddenly, there was a loud knock at the door.

"Who's there?" roared John.

"Listen to me, John Canty!" cried the voice. "The man that you hit with your club last night was Father Andrew! You killed him!"

"God have mercy!" shouted John. "Everyone get up! We must run away before I get caught! Meet me at the cloth maker's shop on London Bridge!"

Everyone knew where London Bridge was. It was a bridge across the River Thames. There were houses and shops and an inn on the bridge, too.

Tom's father grabbed the Prince and ran outside into the street. There were people everywhere! They were dancing and laughing. There were boats with lanterns on the river. Fireworks exploded in the sky. It was a holiday because the Prince of Wales was on his way to the Guildhall in London for a special dinner!

A man grabbed John Canty. "Not so fast!" said the man. "You can't go until you drink a toast to the Prince of Wales!" The man handed Tom's father a huge cup of wine.

John needed both hands just to hold it. When he let go of the Prince to hold the cup, the Prince escaped into the crowd.

"I'll go to the Guildhall!" thought the Prince. "I won't let Tom Canty pretend to be me. I'll show them that *I* am the *real* Prince of Wales. And then I will order them to hang Tom Canty!"

But the crowd at the Guildhall would not let the Prince near the doors.

"You dogs!" he shouted. "I am Edward, Prince of Wales! Let me in!"

The people only laughed and pushed him away.

Then one man stepped forward. He looked like an old soldier. He was tall and he carried a sword, but his clothes were old and faded. His hat had a broken feather.

He spoke to the Prince. "I don't know if you are a prince or not, but you are a brave young man!" he said. "My name is Miles Hendon, and I will protect you."

Miles drew his sword. When another man tried to grab the Prince, Miles struck him with his sword. Now the whole mob attacked Miles.

"They will kill him!" thought the Prince.

Suddenly, a troop of soldiers on horseback rode down the street. "Make way for the King's messenger!" called one of the soldiers.

As everyone jumped out of the way of the horses, Miles grabbed the Prince and carried him away.

The messenger went into the Guildhall. A trumpet played, and everyone in the hall became quiet. "I have news from the palace!" cried the messenger. "King Henry is dead!"

Chapter 5

A New King

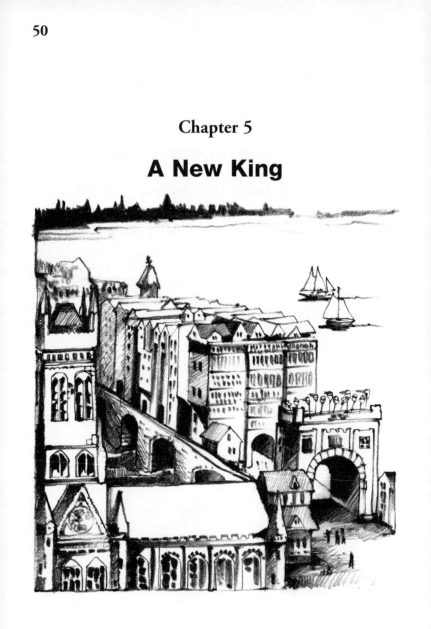

Miles and Edward ran through the alleys and streets of London. People were shouting, "King Henry is dead! Long live King Edward the Sixth!"

"That's me!" Edward thought to himself. "I am King now!" Edward thought about his dead father, and his eyes filled with tears.

Miles took Edward to the inn on London Bridge. But when they got to the bridge, John Canty was there, also! He spotted Edward and tried to grab him.

"So there you are!" cried John. "You won't escape this time, or I'll pound your bones to pudding!"

"Not so fast," Miles demanded. "Who are you?"

"I'm John Canty, and that boy is my son!" said Tom's father as he reached toward Edward.

"That's a lie!" replied the little King. "I will die before I let him touch me!"

Miles drew his sword and pointed it at John Canty. "You won't lay a finger on this boy," said Miles. "Now get out of here before you get hurt!"

Tom's father left, but he was not giving up. "I'll get you, boy," he muttered.

Miles took Edward up to his room in the inn. The room was cold, so Miles gave his coat to the little King. "The boy needs food and sleep," thought Miles.

When a servant from the inn brought food to the room, Edward wanted to wash his hands. He looked at Miles.

"Pour the water," commanded Edward.

Miles was amazed. "First the boy thought that he was the Prince," Miles said to himself. "Now he thinks that he is the new King and I am his servant!" But Miles poured the water anyway.

"Now give me a towel," said the boy.

After drying his hands, Edward sat down at the table. When Miles sat down next to him, Edward shouted at him. "Stand up! How dare you sit when you are near the King!" he cried.

"Well," thought Miles to himself. "He does think that he is the King of England. The boy may be crazy, but I like him, and I will do as he says! I will take care of him and make him well."

Edward wanted to know more about Miles.

"You seem like a noble man," the little King said. "Tell me about yourself."

Miles told Edward about his life. "My father is Sir Richard Hendon. He is a kind and wealthy man. Our home is called Hendon Hall. It is in the countryside," said Miles.

"My mother died when I was a boy," continued Miles. "I grew up with my brother, Hugh, and my cousin, Lady Edith. Lady Edith's father had died, and left his fortune to her. My father wanted Hugh to marry Edith.

But Edith loved *me*, not Hugh,"
explained Miles. "Hugh only pretended
to love Edith so that he could get her
money. Hugh was jealous of me and
Edith, so he made up lies about me,"
said Miles.

"Father believed the lies and
became angry with me," explained
Miles. "He made me join the army.
While I was a soldier, I was captured
and kept in a prison for seven years.
I have just been freed from prison,"
he said.

This story made Edward sad.

"I am going back to Hendon Hall," said Miles. "I want to ask Father to let me marry Lady Edith. I am sure that she has been waiting for me!"

Little King Edward looked at Miles kindly. "You have saved my life," said the King. "So now, as your King, I will grant you a wish."

Chapter 6

A Knight and a Whipping-Boy

Miles didn't really think that Edward could grant a wish, but he didn't want to hurt the boy's feelings. "The boy is serious about this, so I will be serious, also," Miles said to himself.

Miles got down on one knee. "Here is my wish, Sire. For as long as I live, I would like to be allowed to sit down when I am near the King of England."

Edward took Miles's sword and held it up high. "So it shall be," said King Edward.

"You are now *Sir* Miles Hendon. You are a knight in the service of the King!" said Edward. "Now you may sit down with me at my table."

That night, Edward, the new King, slept in the bed, and Miles, the new Knight, slept on the floor. Miles lay across the door so that John Canty could not come in and get the boy.

Early the next morning, Miles went out to buy some better clothes for Edward. When Miles returned, the bed was empty and Edward was gone!

"It's that Canty fellow!" shouted Miles. "He has kidnapped the boy!"

Miles ran down the stairs two at a time. He found a servant downstairs at the inn. "Where is the boy?" demanded Miles.

"He left with a man and another boy," said the servant. He walked over to the door and pointed down the street. "They went that way," he said.

Miles was angry. He ran out the door and down the street to look for Edward.

Meanwhile, Tom Canty was still in the palace. He was asleep and dreaming a wonderful dream. In this dream, he had just found 12 new pennies. He was giving four of the pennies to his mother. She was hugging him and thanking him.

"It is time for Your Majesty to wake up!" said a voice.

Tom groaned. The voice did not belong to his mother. Tom opened his eyes. He was still in the palace.

The good news was that he was no longer Prince of Wales. The bad news was that now he was King of England!

Tom rubbed his eyes. There were more servants than ever in his bedroom. They were here to help him to get dressed. Before he could put on his sock, nine noblemen had to look at the sock, one at a time. Then a tenth nobleman put the sock on Tom's foot. It took a long time for Tom to get dressed.

Tom had to spend all day giving commands and signing papers. It was boring to be a king.

In the afternoon, a new boy came to Tom's room.

"Who are you?" asked Tom.

"I am Humphrey Marlow, Your Majesty," said the boy.

"What do you want?" asked Tom.

"Don't you remember?" asked Humphrey. "I am your whipping-boy."

"My whipping-boy?" asked Tom. "What do you do?"

"*I* get whipped whenever *you* do something bad," replied Humphrey.

Tom said, "Why do *you* get whipped if *I* am bad? Why don't they whip me?"

"They can't whip you," said Humphrey. "No one can whip you, so they whip me instead. When you made mistakes in school last week, I got whipped for them."

Tom felt sorry for the boy. Tom said, "I won't make any more mistakes in school."

"Oh, no!" cried Humphrey. "If you don't make mistakes in school, I will lose my job! I will starve! But now that you are King, you won't have time for school," said Humphrey. "So I will lose my job anyway."

"Don't worry," said Tom. "I will keep studying my books, and I promise to make lots of mistakes."

Tom made Humphrey the Grand
Whipping Boy to the King of England.
The two boys became good friends.
Humphrey was happy because now
he could get whipped every day and
keep his job. Tom was happy because
now he had a friend at the palace.
This friend could tell him the things
that a king should know.

Chapter 7

Stealing a Pig

Tom's father had taken Edward out to a barn in the countryside. A gang of beggars was hiding there. Some of the beggars were young and some were old. They were all dressed in rags. Edward had never seen people like this before.

"Where have you been, John Canty?" asked a man named Ruffler. "We haven't seen you in a long time!"

"I've been in London," said John. "But I killed a priest, so I had to change my name and run away," he said. "You can call me John Hobbs, now."

The gang told John all the news.

A man named Yokel said that he and his family had been chased off their farm. Yokel's mother said she had been whipped because people thought that she was a witch. "I was only trying to help a sick man," she said.

"But the man died and his doctors said that I was a witch," explained Yokel's mother. "So the police whipped me and cut off my ear."

"We are all starving beggars now," said another man. "But begging is against the law."

Edward felt sorry for these people. "The law is not fair!" he cried.

Everyone looked at this new boy. "Who are you?" they asked.

"I am Edward, King of England!" he said.

The people laughed. John laughed also and said, "This is Tom. He's my crazy son. He thinks that he is the King!"

Ruffler spoke again. "We don't care if you are crazy," he said to Edward. "But you must never say that you are the King. We may be beggars, but we still love King Edward. You are not the King."

Another beggar had an idea. "You can be King Foo-Foo," he said. "You can be King Foo-Foo the First!" They were making fun of Edward.

Everyone cheered except Edward and a boy named Hugo. Hugo was jealous of this new boy. So when Ruffler sent Edward and Hugo into a village to steal food, Hugo decided to play a trick on Edward.

Hugo saw a woman walking down the road. She was carrying a basket with a small pig in it. The woman had just bought the pig from the butcher's shop. Hugo sneaked up behind her and grabbed the pig out of her basket. Then he tossed the pig to Edward and yelled, "Run!"

Hugo ran off. But Edward didn't run. He didn't want to steal anything.

The woman did not see Hugo. But she did see her pig and she did see Edward.

"You stole my pig!" she cried. She ran and grabbed Edward.

"Take your hands off me, you fool!" Edward insisted. "I didn't steal it! That other boy stole it!"

A crowd of people gathered around them. No one believed Edward. They were all screaming at him.

Suddenly, a man who had a sword came up. "Let the boy go," said the man. "I will take him to the judge."

It was Miles Hendon!

"Sir Miles," shouted King Edward. "Use your sword!"

"No," said Miles. "We must go to a judge and tell him what has happened."

The woman told her story to the judge, and the judge believed her. He did not believe Edward. "How much is this pig worth?" the judge asked.

"It's worth at least three shillings and eight pence," said the woman.

The judge looked unhappy. "The law says that the thief must be hanged if he steals something that is worth more than 13 pence," he said. "You're saying that your pig is worth more than 13 pence. Do you want this poor boy to be hanged?" asked the judge.

"No, no!" she cried. "Let's forget about the shillings. Let's say that the pig is only worth eight pence."

"Good," said the judge. "Now the boy will not be hanged. He will only have to go to jail."

When the woman left, a policeman followed her outside. "Excuse me," he said. "But I want to buy your pig. Give it to me." The policeman gave her eight pence.

"No!" said the woman. "It's really worth three *shillings* and eight pence!"

The policeman said, "If you don't sell it to me for eight pence, I will tell the judge that you lied. He will put *you* in jail and then he will hang that boy!"

Chapter 8

No Friend at Hendon Hall

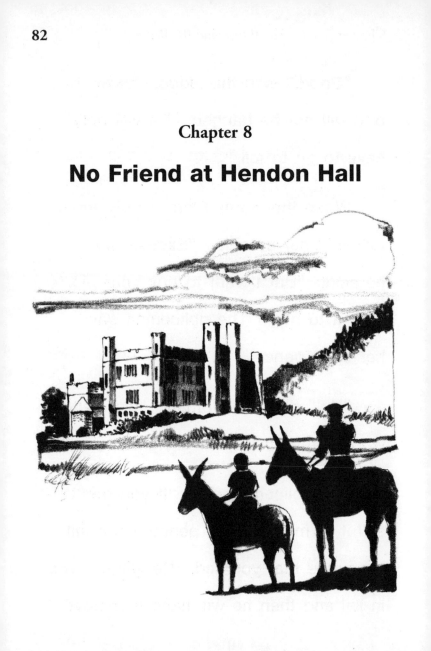

The woman felt angry. She knew that the policeman was cheating her, but she had no choice. She sold him the pig for just eight pence, and went away crying.

Miles had heard the woman talking to the policeman. Miles spoke to the policeman. "I heard you cheating that woman," said Miles. "Now I am going to tell the judge what you did! You broke the law and the law says that *you* should hang!"

The policeman was surprised that Miles had caught him cheating. "Please!" he begged. "What do you want from me?"

Miles said, "I want you to close your eyes, and count slowly to 1,000 so that this boy can escape. Then I want you to give back that pig!"

"I'll do it! I'll do it!" said the policeman.

The policeman closed his eyes, and Miles and the King ran out of town.

For the next three days, Miles and Edward travelled to the village where Miles was born. It was a long way, so they rode on a donkey and a mule.

Edward was happy to be with his friend again. Miles couldn't wait to show Hendon Hall to Edward. It had been ten years since Miles had left home. He was sure that his father, and his sweetheart, Edith, and even his brother Hugh would be glad to see him again.

"We have servants at Hendon Hall," said Miles. "We have 27 servants!" Miles was sure that Edward had never seen a *real* servant before.

When they arrived at Hendon Hall, Miles opened the great front door and found his brother sitting at a table.

"Hugh!" cried Miles. "Tell me that you are glad to see me!"

At first, Hugh looked surprised. Then he stared at Miles.

"Who are you?" asked Hugh. "Do I know you?"

Now Miles was surprised. "I am Miles, your brother!" he said.

"My brother Miles is dead," Hugh replied. "Seven years ago, I got a letter saying that he was killed in the war."

"I'm not dead!" said Miles. "Look at me! Call our father. *He* will know me."

Hugh shook his head. "I cannot call Father. He is dead," said Hugh.

"Dead?" cried Miles. "Then call the old servants. They will know me."

Hugh went out and came back with five servants. Miles remembered them. They had been Hugh's favorite servants, and they had never liked Miles.

"Do you know this man?" Hugh asked them.

The servants shook their heads. They said that they had never seen Miles before.

"Then call Edith," said Miles. "She would *never* forget me."

So Hugh went out again and returned with a beautiful woman. It was Edith. She was walking slowly and looking down at the floor.

Hugh spoke to her. "Do you know this man?" he asked.

Slowly, Edith lifted her head. When she looked into Miles's eyes, her face turned white. "No," she replied. "I do not know him." Then she began to sob and walked out of the room.

"You see! Even my wife does not know you," Hugh told Miles.

"Your *wife?*" cried Miles.

Miles drew his sword and chased Hugh out of Hendon Hall. But soon Hugh returned with the police from the village. Miles tried to fight them, but he could not win. He and the King were taken to jail.

Everything seemed hopeless. Here was the King of England, and no one knew that he was King.

Here was Miles Hendon, and no one around Hendon Hall seemed to remember him.

"It is clear to me that Hugh is the master in this village," Miles muttered to Edward. "No one here dares to speak against him. Not even my dear, sweet Edith."

Chapter 9

In Prison

The jail was dirty and crowded. The food was so awful that Edward could not eat it. Sometimes the guards beat the prisoners, and sometimes the prisoners beat each other. People from the village came to laugh at the prisoners and to call them names. Miles worried that Edward would die in jail.

Everyone in the jail seemed to be there for unfair reasons. A boy was in there because he had stolen a bird and he was sentenced to death.

A girl had stolen a bit of cloth and she was sentenced to be hanged. Two of the other prisoners were women who were only in jail because they had joined the Baptist Church. These women were good to Edward, but soon Edward and Miles were forced to watch them die. The women were tied to a post and burned to death.

The laws that had punished these people were unfair. "I will change these laws and help these poor people when I am back in the palace," Edward promised.

Miles was upset. He had dreamed about returning home for seven years. He felt like a man who had gone out to see a rainbow, but got struck by lightning instead.

One day, an old man came to the jail to see the new prisoners.

"That is my old servant, Blake Andrews!" said Miles to himself.

At first, Blake pretended that he did not know Miles. But when the guards were not looking, Blake spoke to Miles.

"Master Hendon, I know who you are," Blake whispered. "Your brother Hugh also knows who you are, but he is forcing everyone to pretend that they don't know you."

Each day, the old man came back to see Miles and the King. He brought them bits of food and told them what had really happened at Hendon Hall.

"Hugh wrote the letter that said you had been killed in the war," Blake explained to Miles.

"But your father didn't know that," said Blake. "He was old, and when he read that you were dead, he forced Edith to marry Hugh. Now Hugh owns Hendon Hall, and he owns Edith and everyone else in the village. He is terrible to everyone," said Blake. "But don't worry. Edith remembers you and loves you."

"In a few days, King Edward the Sixth will be crowned at Westminster Abbey in London," Blake continued. "Master Hugh will be there."

Edward could not believe his ears! How could they be crowning King Edward the Sixth in London when King Edward the Sixth was sitting here in jail? They would be crowning the wrong person.

At last, Miles and Edward were taken to the judge. The judge punished Miles for pretending to be Miles Hendon, and for attacking his brother Hugh. "You shall sit in the stocks for two hours!" ordered the judge.

Then he spoke to Edward. "This man is no good," said the judge. "A boy like you should stay away from him."

The guards took Miles to the center of the village and locked him in the stocks. Miles sat with his arms and legs locked between boards. People laughed at him and spat at him. One man threw a rotten egg at him.

King Edward could not stand it. "Stop this!" he screamed. "Let this man go! He is my servant, and I am the...!"

Miles was afraid that the boy would be attacked if they heard him speak more. "The boy is crazy!" cried Miles. "Don't listen to him."

Just then, Hugh rode up on his horse. "Give that boy six lashes with a whip!" he called.

"No!" called Miles from the stocks. "Whip me instead!"

Hugh smiled. "That's a good idea," he said. "Let the little beggar go and give this man 12 hard lashings with the whip!"

So the guards took off Miles's shirt and whipped him. The King cried as he watched. When the whipping was over, Edward picked up the whip and touched Miles on his bleeding shoulders. He whispered into Miles's ear. "I, King Edward, make you an Earl," he said.

At last, Miles and the King were allowed to leave. The guards gave Miles back his sword and his donkey and mule. They ordered him out of town and told him never to come back.

"Come quickly, Miles," said Edward. "There is no time to lose! Tomorrow is Coronation Day. We must return to London before they put the crown on the wrong King's head!"

Chapter 10

A King is Crowned

Edward and Miles returned
to London on the night before the
Coronation. People were singing in the
streets. There were so many people
that Miles lost Edward in the crowd!

Meanwhile, Tom Canty had become
used to being King. He had learned
to give orders. He liked to hear the
soldiers call, "Make way for the King!"
He liked having hundreds of servants.
He liked being able to change laws
that were cruel and unfair.

On the day of the crowning, Tom was taken down the River Thames on a boat. When he got to the Tower of London, he was greeted by the sound of cannons. From the Tower, he rode on a beautiful horse in a parade. The parade went all the way to Westminster Abbey. All around him, people cheered, "Long live the King!" As he rode along, Tom tossed coins to the crowd.

"All of this cheering is for me!" he thought to himself.

Suddenly, a woman rushed out of the crowd. She grabbed Tom's leg and began to kiss it. It was his mother!

"Oh, my child!" she cried. "My darling!"

Tom pulled away. Without thinking, he shouted, "I don't know you, woman!"

A guard pushed the woman back into the crowd. Now, Tom felt ashamed and lonely. Suddenly, he wished that he could be back in Offal Court with his mother. But it was too late. There was no way for him to go back now.

At last, the parade arrived at the Abbey. Thousands of poor people stood outside. The rich and noble people were inside. The only empty seat was the King's golden throne.

The long ceremony began. As the ceremony went on and on, Tom's face got very pale. At last, the Archbishop of Canterbury lifted up the crown and held it out over Tom's head.

Suddenly, a boy ran into the Abbey. He was dressed in dirty clothes.

"Stop!" he shouted. "I forbid you to crown that boy. *I* am the real King!"

It was Edward! Someone grabbed him to throw him out, but Tom stood up and shouted, "Let go of him! He is telling the truth. He *is* the King!"

No one moved. No one spoke.

Edward walked proudly toward the throne. Tom bowed down on one knee in front of Edward. "My lord," said Tom. "I shall always be your servant. Put on the crown that is yours!"

The Duke of Hertford was standing next to the boys. He stared at Tom and then at Edward. "They look like twins!" cried the Duke.

Then the Duke turned to Edward and said, "I am the Duke of Hertford. We need to know if you are really the King. Will you answer some questions?"

"I will answer all your questions," Edward replied. "But you are *not* the Duke of Hertford. You are only the *Earl* of Hertford until the true King makes you a duke. *I* am the true king."

The Duke asked Edward questions about the court. He asked him about King Henry, and about other things in the palace. Edward knew the answers to all the questions.

But the Duke was still not sure. "These questions are too easy," he said. "Many people could answer them."

Then suddenly the Duke got an idea. There was one question that Tom had never been able to answer.

"Where is the Great Seal?" asked the Duke. "It has been missing for weeks!"

The Great Seal was a royal tool about the size of a hammer. It was used to print the King's special mark on important papers.

Ever since Tom had come to the palace, the Duke had been asking Tom where it was, but Tom never knew what the Duke was talking about.

"That's easy," said Edward. "The Great Seal is in a secret drawer in the chest by my bed. Press against the nails near the bottom of the chest and the drawer will open."

A lord was sent to look for the Seal.

When he returned, he bowed to Tom and said, "Sire, the Great Seal is not there!"

The Duke shouted, "Take this pauper out of here! He is not Edward the Sixth!"

But again Tom stopped the Duke. "What does this Great Seal look like?" he asked. "Is it made out of metal? Is it round? Does it have a handle? Are there letters on one end of it?"

"Yes, yes, yes," said the Duke. "You know what it looks like, Your Majesty."

"Oh, *that* thing!" cried Tom. "Now I know what you mean. I used the Seal every day. I know where the Seal is, but I did not put it there. *He* did." Tom pointed at Edward. "On the day that you left the palace, you hid the Seal in a new place," Tom continued. "Don't you remember? You ran out of the palace to punish the guards who had hurt me. On the way out, you saw the Seal on the table and you had to hide it quickly."

Edward closed his eyes and thought hard. "Yes!" he cried at last. "I remember now! I hid it in a piece of old armour that is hanging on the wall in my room!"

And that was exactly where they found the Great Seal.

But the King had one more question for Tom. "You said that you used the Great Seal every day yourself. What did you use it for?" asked the King.

"I used it to crack nuts," said Tom.

Everyone laughed. Now they were sure that Tom Canty was not the King.

And so the real Edward was crowned King Edward the Sixth of England.

After he became King, Edward gave Hendon Hall back to Miles. Miles became the Earl of Kent. His brother Hugh left Edith, and went to live in France. Miles and Edith were married at last.

King Edward was also good to Tom. He made Tom a member of his court, and Tom's mother and sisters came to live with him.

King Edward lived only a few years. But while he was King, he always remembered his life as a pauper, and he was a great friend to the poor.

The End

About the Writer

Alan Venable was born in Pittsburgh, Pennsylvania in 1944. After graduating from Harvard, he taught classes in East Africa for several years and traveled in Africa and Asia.

In later years, he studied and taught creative writing and children's literature at several colleges. In addition to his many books in the Start-to-Finish™ series, he has written several books of fiction for children, as well as plays and novels for adults.

Alan lives in San Francisco and is married to Gail Venable, a speech and language clinician and one of the editors of the Start-to-Finish™ series. He and Gail have two children, Morgan and Noe.

About the Writer

Jerry Stemach is a Special Educator who has worked with middle and high school students and adults learning English as a second language for more than 25 years. He has served students with language and learning disabilities as a Speech and Language Pathologist, an Assistive Technology Specialist, and as a Special Education teacher.

Jerry is a member of the Start-to-Finish™ editing team. For the Nick Ford series, he personally visits each city, state, or country that he writes about so that he can tell the story with interesting facts.

Jerry makes his home in the Valley of the Moon in Sonoma County, California with his wife, Beverly, and daughters, Sarah and Kristie.

A Note from the Start-to-Finish™ Editors

This book has been divided into approximately equal short chapters so that the student can read a chapter and take the cloze test in one reading session. This length constraint has sometimes required the authors and editors to make transitions in mid-chapter or to break up chapters in unexpected places.

Some content change is inevitable in order to retell a 400-page book in less than 8,000 words. The authors have had to eliminate some characters and incidents and sometimes manipulate the story's sequence to produce a cohesive story. Every attempt has been made to maintain the essence of the plot, characters, and style of the book.

You will also notice that Start-to-Finish™ Books look different from other high-low readers and chapter books. The text layout of this book coordinates with the other media components (CD and audiocassette) of the Start-to-Finish™ series.

The text in the book matches, line for line and page for page, the text shown on the computer screen, enabling readers to follow along easily in the book. Each page ends in a complete sentence so that the student can either practice the page (repeat reading) or turn the page to continue with the story. If the next sentence cannot fit on the page in its entirety, it has been shifted to the next page. For this reason, the sentence at the top of a page may not be indented, signaling that it is part of the paragraph from the preceding page.

Words are not hyphenated at the ends of lines. This sometimes creates extra space at the end of a line, but eliminates confusion for the struggling reader.